Timid Tim and The Bright Red Toolbox go to Murrumburrah.

John O' Shea

Illustrations by Stephen Stanley

ISBN 978 1 300 89308 0

Email: johnstoolbox@hotmail.com

www.stancartoons.com

Produced with the support of the Whyalla Writers' Group

TIMID TIM and the *Bright Red Toolbox* go Murrumburrah.

Author's introduction

This is my third anti-bullying book of Timid Tim. Tim is growing up fast, the hormones of puberty are really kicking in. I will dedicate this book to the people in this world that need a second chance to understand their bad choices and the flow on effect of those decisions. Life has become so complicated, sometimes well intended actions have the opposite effect.

Readers will experience a special moment in Tim's life, as he learns that the *Bright Red Toolbox* is required to teach him how to get his life on track. Tim, not quite 15 years old, has all the traits of typical boys his age. Bill, Tim's dad. is added to the series. Bill and Tim's mother Julie divorced when Tim was a small boy of 8 years old. Tim became withdrawn and timid while the divorce proceeded, especially without having a father figure once his mum gained full custody.

Each chapter will allow readers to follow Tim, his friends and family, as they struggle with real life obstacles. Sharing some of my own life's experience, I will describe the ramifications of wrong choices. The stories are fictitious, with no reference to real people, but based on general behaviour typical of families with offspring in this age group.

New characters will need the help of the *Bright Red Toolbox*, believing they are above the law of the rules applicable in school and out of school activities. Tim will be starting year nine at Murrumburrah High School in the twin town of Harden. Will the *Bright Red Toolbox* have to come to his aid?

My dream is to allow the stories and books I write, to educate ordinary public, from all walks of life, that just because we(people diagnosed with ADHD and Bipolar disorder) might think and act/react a bit differently, doesn't necessarily mean we are disabled. In a lot of situations, people like us that see things from a different perspective may have superior problem-solving skills.

This book delivers a very positive message of forgiveness, unconditional love, and more importantly, anyone can change their bad behaviour, but only if they own their mistakes, by that I mean, be accountable for their mistakes or wrongdoing and seek out proper professional help. Only with professional guidance can anyone successfully change their thought processes, so they don't fall back into their bad habits.

I took this photo in 1982 of the house our family lived in Murrumburrah before we moved to Adelaide in 1962. I was two years old.

Timid Tim, needs a bit of his own medicine.

One Saturday morning, Tim woke up feeling different than he had felt before. At 14 and a half years old, the hormones of puberty were throwing confusion at him.

This confusion brought back the same anxiety and negative feelings he experienced years earlier facing bullies like Big Bad Bruce. Readers can better understand the feeling by reading my first book "Timid Tim and the Bright Red Toolbox."

Tim grabbed some of the clothes that were strewn across the floor, giving them a quick sniff. 'They'll do,' he thought as he dressed himself. He plopped himself down in the lounge room chair. Tim's mum, Julie asked: "Have you taken the rubbish out like I asked last night, Tim?"

Completely ignoring his mother, Tim switched on the Nintendo Switch game and started playing his Favorite game, 'Mario Kart'. Before Julie could ask Tim again, the council garbage truck could be heard emptying the bins in the street. Tim knew he had forgotten to take the bin out to the footpath before the truck came; he thought the truck was not due for another half hour and wanted to try and achieve the next level on his game before taking the bin out.

Tim's mum stormed into the lounge room, "TURN THAT GAME OFF, NOW."

Tim looked up. "Mum, I just need to finish this race. I am winning and there are only two laps to go." Julie was having trouble understanding the change in Tim's attitude. In a few short months, Tim had gone from a helpful, calm, and obedient boy to an arrogant, argumentative teenager. It was Tim's turn to get angry as Julie leaned over the television entertainment unit and switched the game off at the power point. Tim let out a few rude comments, stomped through the house to his bedroom, and slammed the door so hard

the whole house shook. Julie slumped down on the couch, tears running down her cheeks in despair.

Tim's feelings were similar however. He was in a state of confusion. Not wanting to be the teenager he was turning out to be. His running legs behaved like a galloping giraffe, and the pain in his legs sometimes made it hard for him to sleep, so he woke up grumpy. Another problem was that he missed his mates. Clive, his best friend, was still in the outback, going there for the Christmas holidays. He was not due back until the school holidays finished in two weeks. Wiping tears from his eyes, he heard his mum knock lightly on the door. "Come in mum, I'm sorry", apologised Tim. Julie tried to understand that Tim was just like most teenagers, but it didn't make it any easier to cope.

Once Julie was in the bedroom, it was impossible not to miss the dirty clothes on the floor. "How can you live in this mess, Tim?" she said as she started to pick up some of the clothes off the floor. Well, that just started Tim off again. "Don't touch anything, I'll clean it tomorrow, now get out of my room."

By the time Julie had reached the kitchen, there was a knock at the door. Their next-door neighbour, Mr. Harper had heard the commotion and had come to check that everything was okay. Julie opened the door, "Hi, Mr. Harper, we must have been loud, it's the first time you've knocked on my door."

"Is everyone okay Mrs. Bowman?" Before Julie had time to reply, Tim had come out of his room, and looking Mr. Harper directly in the eyes screamed, "Yes mate, it's none of your bees wax, now piss off, and mind your own business."

Julie's ex-husband, Bill, Tims dad, lived interstate on the Murimboola Creek in Murrumburrah, New South Wales. Bill had been out of the picture since the divorce, dealing with his own traumatic injustices. Bill had finally got his life on track, although finding a suitable partner has been beyond his capability. Employment was also becoming an issue. Bill had the capacity to perform the tasks required, but meeting selection criteria would have entailed divulging private information that Bill was not willing to share. Call it coincidence, or power from above, but Julie decided to try the only phone number she knew, to contact Bill.

One quiet afternoon, Tim was out riding his bike, so Julie used the opportunity to try Bill's number. Bill had just arrived home, from another rejected job interview, then Bill heard his mobile ring. He picked up the phone off the kitchen table. No caller ID showed while buzzing. His finger hovered over the 'reject call button', but Bill swiped the green. "Hello, William speaking," Bill said in an official tone in case it was from an employment opportunity.

Julie responded as calmly as her emotions would allow. "Bill, It's Julie, are you free for a little chat?"

Bill could sense the serious nature of the call. "What's up Julie? How is Tim now he's a teenager?"

Julie decided to get straight to the point: "Tim has grown from a shy, vulnerable boy to a teenager of confidence and great character, but I believe he needs a dad to instil some authority which I don't seem to be able to provide."

Bill took his time answering his ex-wife. "Sorry Julie, I kept you hanging on the phone. I was quite shocked to get a call from you after six and a half years." Bill went on to say: "I do want to help. I'm not sure how yet, but can you give me your number as it's not showing up on my phone?"

Julie provided Bill with the contact details with the call cut short by Tim arriving home on his bike. Tim seemed in a better mood as he came in through the back door. "Hi mum, would you like me to put the kettle on?" Tim asked.

"That would be nice Tim, maybe we can start afresh."

Sitting down on the lounge together, sipping on hot coffee in a relaxed atmosphere for the first time in months. Tim and his mum kept the conservation to idle chatter at first, then Julie asked: "Would things be better if you had your dad or a father figure around to talk on teenage boy growing up issues?"

Tim looked a bit bewildered at first, then he asked, "Do you know where dad is?"

Well now it was Julie's turn to think carefully before answering Tim. She then replied "Tim, while I have tried my best to be a good mother, there are times I feel completely unsure of the best way to talk to you without another screaming match." Julie then went on to say: "I called the last mobile number I had for your dad, and he answered, telling me he is living in country NSW and is interested in making contact with you."

Tim had trouble processing so much information in his confused adolescent brain. He said to his mother: "You are a great mother, mum. Dad's been away from us for so long. My last memories of him are of the arguments between you and dad during the divorce."

Both Tim and his mother finished their coffee, then they both stood up, with emotions building up, little tears forming in their eyes, they shared a wonderful hug. Tim finished the conversation while his arms were still wrapped around his mother, "How about we sleep on it tonight, and chat about it tomorrow?"

Tim went to bed early that night, Julie received a text from her ex-husband outlining his contact details. Opening her laptop while sitting up in bed, Julie googled the twin-town address. At first, she mis-spelled the rather large name, 'Murrumburrah-Harden'. Julie let out a giggle as she learnt Murrumburrah High School is actually in Harden. Julie did wonder why Bill lived in the Murrumburrah part of town with an almost ghost town population of 78 at the last census in 2021, while the Harden side housed 1,900 residents. 'Oh well, not my problem' she thought, closing her laptop, and switching off the light hoping for a sound sleep.

Conversation progressed over the next couple of days. Tim seemed a little happier while chatting with his dad. They even touched base on options of meeting up. Tension between Tim and his mother had improved a little, but Julie was beginning to worry about the speed of the father-son relationship. A couple of nights later, Julie reminded Tim, "You need to put your dirty clothes on to wash."

Tim replied with: "I'll do it a bit later. I'm about to have a shower, but don't go in my room."

Sensing Tim was hiding something, Julie became a bit suspicious. Julie noticed the door to Tim's bedroom was open and dirty clothes were all over the floor. Deciding she was in charge, not Tim, Julie picked up the dirty clothes. A packet of cigarettes fell out of a pair of jeans Tim had been wearing.

Just as Julie picked up the cigarettes, Tim stormed into the room. "Get out of my room, I need my privacy."

Confiscating the smokes, Julie walked out of the room. "We will talk about this later, Tim."

Slamming the door, Tim swore under his breath as he got dressed.

Julie was at the end of her tether; she did not know how to bring up the subject of the cigarettes and ongoing sneakiness with Tim. While pondering the options, Julie's phone buzzed with the ID 'Tim's Dad' as the caller. "Hello Bill" she answered, but before he could even get a word in Julie continued: "I need help Bill. Tim is getting out of control, and I don't know how to handle his moods or finding out he is smoking".

Bill finally had a chance to catch his breath replying: "I'm sorry that you're having to struggle with Tim's antics on your own. It doesn't seem fair". Bill really wanted to help Julie bring Tim up during the turbulent teenage years but was not sure how to assist due to his limited income and housing issues. Bill did throw Julie a lifeline; "Julie, would you like Tim to come over here for a while? It might teach him that the grass is not necessarily greener on the other side of the fence, so to speak."

Julie wasn't expecting Bill to provide such a suggestion, especially as Julie had full custody ever since the traumatic events leading up to their divorce. Julie finished the conversation, leaving all options on the table. "Thanks for your thoughtful offer, it might give us all something to look into, hopefully finding a resolution to an expanding problem".

Readers who have experienced the positive impact of the *Bright Red Toolbox*, from the previous books must be wondering when its use will be introduced to this chapter. I can assure you all, 'the excitement is about to start'. Frustration had increased for Tim as he found out on social media that one of his best friends, Clive, the indigenous boy in the previous book, was going to be home-schooled in the outback while going through cultural initiation.

Tim's attitude was deteriorating by the day, like an out-of-control train heading for derailment. One morning, the *Bright Red Toolbox* decided it was time to teach Tim a lesson, utilizing the drone like propellers, the *Bright Red Toolbox* moved quietly from the bookshelf. Hovering very close to the sleeping teenager, using the foghorn voice device, the *Bright Red Toolbox* yelled "TIM, GET UP." Well, Tim got up alright, he jumped out of bed, nearly soiling his boxers, ran across the room, tripped on the pile of clothes on the floor, landing seated in the gaming computer chair, completely unsure what was happening.

Julie heard the commotion and knocked on Tim's door. "What's going on in there, Tim?"

"Don't come in here, mum, I'm just cleaning my room," he lied.

"Oh, okay then." She replied. What Tim didn't know; was that Julie had been putting the final arrangements in place for Tim to live with his dad for a while to see what happened.

The *Bright Red Toolbox* wasn't finished yet, using the foghorn with the volume lowered to a bit more than a whisper: "A bit of advice, young man. You had better get your act together, ditch the cigarettes and anything else you are afraid of your mother seeing."

The *Bright Red Toolbox* was starting to have the desired effect on Tim. Later, while making his mum and himself a cuppa, he said: "Mum, I know an apology is not enough to make up for the way I've been behaving, but I am truly sorry."

The good mother Julie was, provided the perfect unconditional love message. "Tim, all is forgiven, all I ever want is the best for you."

The discussions were interrupted by the sound of a whirring sound coming from Tim's bedroom, the *Bright Red Toolbox* came flying slowly through the doorway of the bedroom towards the seated mother and son.

Julie had listened to the stories Tim had described of the power of the *Bright Red Toolbox*, but this was the first time she witnessed it firsthand. The *Bright Red Toolbox* settled itself down on the table, Tim was in awe as he decided to open the *Bright Red Toolbox*. Tim said, "Look mum, there's an envelope addressed to both of us inside."

Over in NSW, Bill had tried to prepare for the possibility of Tim coming over to stay for a while, but with limited savings and no positive employment prospects, Bill was unable to see a way forward. A local and very kind lady, Jean Wiseman, saw a social media post asking for unwanted bedroom furniture to help Bill accommodate Tim. Call It a miracle or the power above, there was no evidence of who submitted the social media post. Readers of my books would easily understand the plea for bedroom furniture to be the power of the *Bright Red Toolbox*.

Jean Wiseman had organized a friend to collect a full bedroom suite, no longer needed as the kids had grown up and left home. Graham Dennison, a close friend of both Jean Wiseman and Bill Bowman, reversed into the narrow driveway of Bill's Neill St cladded cottage. Bill met Graham in the driveway, "What's all this?" asked Bill.

Graham replied with a big grin on his face. "A lovely lady friend of mine, Jean Wiseman, saw a social media post and decided to help."

Bill was in shock. Surprised and grateful all at the same time, responding with, "WOW, I don't know what to say."

Graham said, "A sincere thank you is all that's needed," as he carried the single bed ends up the wooden steps leading up to the decked front veranda. Bill hadn't had time to clean out the spare room, so the bedroom suite had to be stacked neatly on the front veranda.

Julie carefully lifted the envelope from the *Bright Red Toolbox.* "What do you think is in the envelope, Tim?"

"I have no idea really, except to say that It could be something positive towards a resolution for my behaviour."

Julie handed Tim the envelope. "You can do the honours."

Tim opened up the envelope and found two tickets inside. Tim looked at the top one. "It's a plane ticket from Adelaide to Sydney for both of us in a weeks' time." Handing the economy class ticket to his mum, Tim looked at the second ticket. "I'm a bit confused. This ticket is only for you to return to Adelaide. What's going to happen with me?"

Before Julie could answer, her phone indicated Bill was calling. "Hello Bill, how can I help?"

"Julie, some friends have organized the bedroom furniture needed if Tim is to come over for a trial period."

"Bill, I am not sure how to explain this, but Tim's *Bright Red Toolbox* has supplied flight travel tickets for Tim and me to Sydney and for me to return home in about a week."

Julie's phone had been on speaker, so Tim was able to hear the whole conversation and he was not happy. Tim joined the conversation with: "Are you both saying that what started out as just a suggestion, the *Bright Red Toolbox* provided the transport and second-hand furniture, so I have to move to some town with a name longer than the encyclopedia?"

Now it was time for the *Bright Red Toolbox* to speak through the foghorn, also at low volume: "Tim needs to be taught a lesson for his bad behaviour, Julie needs a break from the rude teenager, and finally, Bill deserves a chance to bond with his son who hasn't been part of his life for nearly seven years". After the *Bright Red Toolbox* had finished delivering the message, the lid closed, and it became just like any normal toolbox.

Although Tim, Julie and Bill were shocked by the outcome put together by the *Bright Red Toolbox*, they all seemed to agree that the idea had merit. Tim might be able to appreciate his mother more, since he faces tough challenges not experienced before.

The Bright Red Toolbox at Purple Lips Café

The seven days until departure day went fast, Tim was not sure he liked the *Bright Red Toolbox's* decision, providing tickets and furniture for Tim's move to Murrumburrah, NSW. Julie had her own concerns, knowing how much she would miss her son, but also understanding the difficulties coping with Tim's growing up years. Over in NSW, Bill has been busy getting the room ready for Tim. He was also showing signs of anxiety for the challenges the next few months could bring. The two-bedroom cottage would struggle to accommodate the father and son, let alone the few days Julie may stay while Tim settled in.

Julie gave up negotiating with Tim regarding what to pack, although she did understand why Tim was adamant the *Bright Red Toolbox* would be included. Julie bought a few cheap suitcases at a local market while she would travel light, using her luggage weight allowance of 23kg of checked-in baggage for Tim's additional items. The *Bright Red Toolbox* had to be checked in with a special pre-flight declaration order to be anti-terrorist compliant. 'Just imagine the panic if security staff set off an alarm, thinking the *Bright Red Toolbox* was a terrorist threat.'

The day of departure arrived. "Tim, are you ready?" Julie asked as the taxicab pulled up outside.

Tim yelled out, "Just a minute mum," then he opened the bedroom door, dragging the bulky suitcase and carrying the *Bright Red Toolbox* with the declaration order attached. The twenty-five-minute taxi drive to the airport was a rather quiet one. Both Julie and Tim found communication difficult. Tim had trouble expressing his sorrow for his disrespectful behaviour. Julie, on the other hand, had trouble dealing with Tim's attitude and how her ex-husband would cope with his outbursts. Surprisingly, Tim started the conversation. "Mum, I'm sorry for how I have treated you. Will you forgive me?"

"Of course, I will forgive you, Tim. There's nothing to forgive really, you're just a kid trying to deal with the pressures of growing up." In the final stages of the taxi ride, they both chatted cheerfully, with Julie laughing as she said: "I wonder if the kids at Murrumburrah High School, are prepared for the power of the *Bright Red Toolbox?*" As I write this story, I wonder if Tim too was ready for the challenges ahead.

The flight from Adelaide to Sydney went without a hitch, and being his first flight, Tim acted like a five-year-old as the Boeing 737-300 blasted off into the sky. Julie relaxed while sipping on a glass of chardonnay and snacking on the complimentary cheese and crackers. Tim scoffed down the free can of Coke, his cheeks bulging from cramming potato chips by the handful into his mouth. Once the aircraft reached cruising altitude, Tim searched the internal aircraft Wi-Fi for information on take-off, cruising, and landing speed. Fascinated by the results, allowing for a few variables, wind, weight, and ambient temperature, the B737-300 needs nearly 2.5km of runway to reach take-off speed of 270km/h. Tim got so excited reading the data, he asked:

"Mum, did you know we are cruising at over 10 thousand metres, or 10 kilometres high and over 800kp/h?"

Julie's reply was predictable. "I am pleased that you are in a good mood, Tim, but statistics like that have the opposite effect. They scare me, so I would rather you kept those facts to yourself," but she said it with a smile on her face.

The motel room Julie had prebooked included a balcony overlooking Sydney Harbour for the overnight stay. Bill would collect them about lunchtime for the nearly 350km drive to Murrumburrah. Tim wasn't impressed having to share the one room with his mother. The single bed in the corner didn't provide enough privacy. Although the aircraft landed smoothly, they were delayed due to the *Bright Red Toolbox* having been put onto a different flight. Fortunately, the delay was only a few hours and to compensate, the airline provided a complimentary lunch with plenty of free coffee and soft drinks. Later, Julie lay down for an afternoon siesta, trying to block out the noise Tim was making playing video games on his phone.

That evening, they both watched the sunset from the rooftop restaurant, the spectacular view might have been free, but the food almost blew the budget.

Bill called in the morning, suggesting a slight change in plans. "Julie, because the motel is close to central train station, can you travel by train to Penrith, it only cost a few dollars each, leaves every ten minutes and takes about 50 minutes. It will save me two or three hours."

"That should be ok, Bill. Can we meet up at the Penrith train station for lunch?" Julie replied.

"Rightio. Can't wait to see Tim. I'd better hit the road."

Tim was grumpy after staying up late playing his video games. "Tim, you need to move a bit faster," Julie said while lugging the heaviest suitcase along the train terminal looking for platform eight. Tim had a backpack on his back, the *Bright Red Toolbox* in his left hand and dragging the slightly lighter suitcase, grumbling all the way.

The train ride was far superior to the old rattlers experienced on the Adelaide lines; they were on time for a start. After their arrival, Tim let out a laugh as Julie found a table at the Purple Lips Café on the corner of Station

22

Road. Julie asked: "What's so funny?" as she hadn't noticed the actual name of the café, only looking for a suitable table. Julie also had a chuckle. Choosing a café with such a name, especially after texting Bill with the details.

Tim placed the *Bright Red Toolbox* in the middle of the table. Bill walked through the door of Café, spotted the *Bright Red Toolbox*, and gave a wave before joining Julie and Tim at the table. "Hi, dad," Tim said, standing up and putting his hand out to shake hands, but Bill had other ideas.

"Come here, son" he said, opening up his arms. Tim's reaction was positive and they both embraced warmly. Julie was pleased with Tim's reaction. She also gave Bill a hug, but maybe not so passionately.

While seated, enjoying the relaxed atmosphere of the Purple Lips Café, a pair of older teenagers burst through the door. Both were wearing hoodies, but the tall skinny lad was already at the counter waving a machete. Audrey, the elderly owner, wearing iconic purple lipstick which complemented the namesake of the Purple Lips Café, let out a loud scream. The shorter stocky teenager jumped the counter and immediately began to help himself to the open cash register. Bill, Julie, and Tim looked at each other, wondering what to do as they were the only customers at the Purple Lips Cafe. Time seemed to be moving in slow-motion. While they stared at each other, the *Bright Red Toolbox* activated it's rotor-blades, quietly lifting off the centre of the table.

The *Bright Red Toolbox* locked the front entrance doors by flicking the latch with the 'Lever extension,' a new addition to the *Bright Red Toolbox's bag of tricks.*

Julie also swung into action, calling the Police on OOO, the emergency number in Australia. The two teenage thugs finished tormenting Audrey the owner and headed for the locked door. Still brandishing the machete, the teenagers looked very dangerous. Their hands were full of the stolen property. The *Bright Red Toolbox* swung into action, buzzing very close to the skinny lad waving the machete.

"What the hell?" the skinny lad yelled, noticing the *Bright Red Toolbox* for the first time. At the same time, the stocky teenager tripped over the chair the *Bright Red Toolbox* had moved as an obstacle for the rushing thug. The *Bright Red Toolbox* knocked the machete out of the skinny lad's hand. Fortunately, the machete landed safely on the floor. By the time the bandits reached the front door, the Police were on the other side, trying to open the locked door.

The element of excitement was about to explode. The *Bright Red Toolbox* used the lever extension to unlock the front door of the Purple Lips Café, while dodging the waving arms of the two idiotic teenage robbers. Tim had been commentating on the entertainment, gloating with the fact that his *Bright Red Toolbox* had spoilt the robbery plans of the two teenagers. They all continued to finish their fabulous lunch, realizing the danger was over. Two burly armed Police Officers rushed through the unlocked front doors.

One Officer, with Glock revolver drawn ordered: "On the floor, NOW!"
The other Officer quickly handcuffed the two teenage fools.

The robbers in handcuffs were then marched outside, and into the
waiting Paddy Wagon. The *Bright Red Toolbox* returned to the centre of the
table. Audrey the owner, was so grateful to receive the stolen goods back,
after the Police had taken photos and fingerprints for evidence, she
announced: "Coffee's on the house, before you head off."

Timid Tim, meets Vaping Victora in NSW

The road trip to Murrumburrah/Harden went without further interruption. Bill was proud of his Blue BA, 2005 Ford Falcon XR6. It had plenty of power to tackle the 'Great Dividing Range.' Tim enjoyed chatting about cars with Bill as the big powerful Ford roared around a tight corner within the recommended speed sign. The 18-inch low profile tyres gripped the road like superglue. Julie, seated in the back, as Tim had commandeered the front seat before Julie had time to protest, yelled out: "Bill, can you slow down a bit, I have to hang on to the grab handle?"

Bill turned the loud music down on the upgraded Kenwood stereo head-unit, mistaking speed for sound. "Is that better?" Bill said, negotiating yet another tight corner.

"I said slow down, but I am glad the AC/DC is not so loud."

Bill replied, "The road will straighten out soon, but I will be more responsible and take the corners at a more respectable speed."

"Here we are," Bill said as he pulled up outside the Neill St cottage. Tim was just waking up after snoozing, due to the late afternoon sun on his face. Julie got out of the car, taking in all the surroundings, including the small cottage. "Help your mother with the luggage," Bill said after opening the large boot.

"Okay dad," replied Tim while unloading the heaviest suitcase. Julie carried the lighter suitcase and the carry-on backpack. Bill helped Tim as he struggled with the heaviest item up the old wooden steps of the front veranda. Bill showed Tim the small bedroom he had set up for him. "I know it's not much, but a big improvement on what it was."

"It's okay, dad, I can add my own touch. It's great, really." Tim went over to where his mum and dad were chatting and said, "I think I owe you both a hug."

Julie was first to wake up the next morning, having had a restless night on the pull-out sofa in the lounge. She could hear Bill snoring through the thin walls, which brought back memories of their married life. Tim had slept well, which had been a surprise after all the excitement of the previous day. Stumbling through the hallway to the primitive bathroom, Tim saw his mother in the kitchen and asked, "What's for breakfast?"

Julie had already found eggs, bacon and the loaf of fresh bread bought along the drive the day before. "Wake your dad up after you get back from the bathroom and I'll put on some bacon and eggs."

Bill followed Tim into the kitchen. "Well, I haven't had breakfast cooked for me since we were together."

"Don't get any ideas, I'm still leaving on the XPT train tomorrow."

It was a busy day, checking Tim into the Murrumburrah High school in Harden. Tim's Yr-9 home-group teacher, Mr Harding explained the origin of the twin towns. The early pioneers of the original settlement on the banks of Murrimboola creek named the town Murrumburrah, which later became Harden, named after the railway siding. The correct name of the twin town is now 'Harden-Murrumburrah'. Julie and Bill went to a local bakery for coffee and cake, while Tim sat a pre-entrance test for High School due to coming from interstate.

Tim passed the test, finishing just as his mum and dad returned. Mr. Harding advised all three of them that Tim would be able to start in three days, on the Monday. He went on to say that School uniforms were mandatory. Knowing Bill's unemployment situation, Mr. Harding was able to provide some good second-hand items through the 'High School Uniform Recycling Scheme.'

The next day, Tim was a bit emotional as his mother waited for the XPT train at the Harden Station. Julie had been surprised at the $39 one-way concession fare. The train left twice daily for Central Station in Sydney, taking four and a half hours, quicker than Bill's powerful Ford Falcon XR6 and without the traffic issues.

Farewell hugs and last words were interrupted by the loud blast from the horn of the XPT (Express Passenger Train). The XPT was introduced by the NSW government in 1982, to service same day passenger travel to Sydney. Each train has two, 12-cylinder turbo diesel locomotives, developing 1495kw of power each, one at the front pulling and another at the rear pushing.

Julie told Tim to be a good boy and she would call each Sunday. Bill said, "Don't worry Julie, I'll keep him in line, or he might get the other end of the stick," chuckling as he saw the look on Tim's face.

Tim spent most of Saturday, organising his room. Bill handed Tim a micro-fibre cloth to give the *Bright Red Toolbox*, the shine it deserved after the job it performed at the Purple Lips Café. Tim became a bit frustrated cleaning the bare wooden floorboards, the broom creating dust clouds that seemed to settle back down on the swept floor. Bill came back into the bedroom after hearing Tim swearing loudly. "Tim, don't worry about the floor, the Vacuum cleaner broke while getting the room ready, I'll borrow one during the week." Bill then added, "I have a bit of a surprise for you in the small garden shed, let's go and have a look." Tim jumped up from the bed, instantly feeling much better. Bill noticed Tim looking at the overgrowth of onion weed, particularly as they got closer to the shed. "Yeah, Tim, it's a bit of a mess out the back. But it will give you something to do if you get bored on the weekend." Tim laughed, adding the sarcastic remark: "I'll be too busy catching up on homework, or playing my video games."

"Open up the shed, Tim," said Bill. Struggling with the rickety old door, Tim finally got the door open. The surprise didn't need any more explaining, the mid-day sun shone directly on the new mountain bike. Tim was speechless as his eyes focused on the bright blue frame, letting out a "WOW" as he noticed the front suspension forks, disc brakes front and rear. Tim was not a huggie type teenager, typical of most boys his age. The emotion and gratitude however encouraged Tim to display a rare father-son loving moment. "Thanks dad" Tim said, as he hugged the father that he was still slowly getting to know.

"That's alright Tim, it might make up for some of the years I haven't been there when you needed me."

That night, Julie called to say she had arrived back at Oxtail Creek "Tim, I hope you have a great first day at school tomorrow, I will miss, not being there".

Tim said, "Thanks mum, it will be different without you there." Then Tim starting to tell him mum about the bright blue bike, by describing in detail, the gears, brakes, and suspension.

Julie interrupted. "Tim, that's great, but I have no idea about those things, have a great day tomorrow. Now can I talk to your dad?"

"Yeah mum, here he is", passing the phone to Bill. Bill and Julie chatted for a few minutes, Tim yelled out, "I'm going to bed now, dad, see you in the morning before I head off to school."

"Goodnight Tim," said Bill, after telling Julie to hang-on for a second.

Tim woke up fresh the next morning as he had slept well, even with the excitement and uncertainty of starting a new school. Tim was happy, knowing he had his bright blue bike to ride to school. Bill joined Tim for a hearty breakfast including cereal, orange juice and vegemite on toast. "You look like a fine young man in that school uniform," praised Bill.

Tim replied, "the uniform fits perfectly, you wouldn't even think it was second hand." Bill smiled at Tim as his son continued. "I'm missing mum, but really want to improve my attitude and make you and mum proud."

Bill replied, "Tim, you have already made a huge difference in your attitude, but you'd better get going before you're late on the first day, and don't forget your helmet."

"Thanks for reminding me," Tim said as he rushed out the door.

Tim arrived at the Murrumburrah High School on Smith Street in the Harden side of the twin-town. Locking his bright blue bike in the designated bicycle shed, Tim went looking for the 9-C classroom. Tim was distracted by a female student looking at him, he found her attractive, but he had this conflicting emotion that almost scared him. Mr. Harding, the home group teacher, interrupted Tim's confusion. "Welcome, Tim, the classroom is this way." Mr Harding then instructed the girl that had mesmerised Tim.

"Victoria, you need to hurry up, you are never on time, how about you help out our new student, Tim Bowman settle-in?"

Victoria replied with an un-enthusiastic, "I suppose, if I really have to."

Tim did feel a bit like 'a fish out of water' in the new class. Finding a single desk, centrally located, Mr. Harding invited Tim to the front for a formal introduction and welcome. Tim blushed a bright red as he looked how attentive the other 24 students were as he gave a brief impromptu introduction; they clapped loudly after Tim's introduction.

Tim found a quiet table near the quadrangle, enjoying his lunch in the warm autumn sunshine. Victoria strolled over to Tim's table, "Mind if I join you?"

Tim was a bit hesitant, before answering. "Yeah, that's okay." Being a bit inquisitive, he noticed that Victoria didn't have any lunch with her. "Not hungry today?" he asked.

"Not really, I am trying to lose a bit of weight." she replied. They chatted a bit more before the bell rang for them to go back to class, "I am just going to sneak behind the building for a vape, don't tell the teachers please."

"It's not a good idea, but you don't have to worry about me," said Tim. During the afternoon lessons, Tim noticed that Victoria had excused herself many times.

That evening, Bill asked Tim how the first day went, Tim explained the embarrassment of the introduction, then he said, "The studies are about my level, but I was given more homework than I expected."

"Well, I suppose that gets you out of doing the dishes, you'd better get cracking on the homework." Tim said goodnight to his dad, deciding not to discuss the issue of vaping.

The next few days were more of the same. Victoria seemed to be the only student taking steps to make friends. Tim wondered if he was being avoided because of spending time with Victoria. "Why are you trying to lose weight? I'm a bit worried about the damage vaping is doing to your body and mindset."

Victoria burst into tears, yelling, "Mind your own business," before running to her hiding spot behind the building to vape some more. Tim felt hurt, he had just upset the only person who had made contact with him. Checking the time, and seeing that there were a few minutes left before the bell, Tim quietly snuck around to the rear of the building. Tim was able to witness Victoria exchange money for a packet of vapes. What shocked Tim more, was that the seller was a middle-aged man, similar looking to the school gardener. Thinking to himself, he wondered how this sort of activity could go unnoticed during breaks in lesson time.

A few days later, he shielded his eyes from the early morning sun as he awoke. Shining bright through a gap between the faded old-fashioned curtains, the rays were directed on to the dusty, not so *Bright Red Toolbox*. Looking at his watch, then at the *Bright Red Toolbox*, he began to think it was about time he gave it good clean. No time before school today, but the weekend started tomorrow, Tim made a mental note to clean it then.

Victoria Struggles with Vaping Addiction

On this sunny Friday, Victoria started to open up to Tim about the addiction to vapes and the strain it had on her mental health. It had started out as a dare, a bit of a joke with a girl last year in the 8th grade class, to try a cigarette. Like countless young teenagers, for many generations, sneaking the odd OP 'other persons' cigarette behind the toilet block or sports shed, was considered cool. *Writing this paragraph, reminds me of my first smoke, aged 12, still in primary school, Frank, one of my few friends, had a packet of '10' Glendale, which cost only 25 cents.*

Victoria went on to explain that the culprit, named Sandra, kept offering her smokes every day, increasing the amount every few days. Sandra had kept saying, "Here, have a few, just pay me back one day." Victoria had always said, "I don't get much money, I don't think I'll ever be able to pay you back."

The end of lunch bell rang. "We can keep chatting after school today, dad usually goes to the pub on a Friday afternoon, for a couple of schooners (same size as pints in South Australia).

"No worries," shouted Victoria as she raced around the back of the building for her usual vape before class.

After school, Tim met up with Victoria at the nearby park and asked about Sandra. "How come Sandra is not at school this year?"

"Sandra kept feeding me the smokes until I was totally addicted," Victoria replied. She continued with, "Sandra came after the money for the smokes, bullying me every day. I started shoplifting to pay my debt and continued supply." Sandra and Victoria had been caught shoplifting together. They had stolen six cartons of cigarettes from a delivery van, while the driver was inside a fuel service station. The driver had been a bit negligent, forgetting to close the lock properly on the rear barn doors. The girls were caught, because the CCTV camera at the rear of the service station clearly showed their faces and school uniform. Victoria said, "The police came to my door a few days later while Sandra was visiting my house." Victoria didn't know that Sandra was carrying a weapon, a replica gel-blaster pistol, which is illegal without a gun licence in Australia. Victoria continued; "The police searched the house, they didn't find the hidden smokes, but Sandra was charged for the concealed gel-blaster." Sandra had blamed all the wrongdoing on Victoria.

Tim Interrupted again, "But that still doesn't explain why Sandra stopped coming to

Murrumburrah High School?"

"Sandra's parents decided to move away because of my supposed *bad influence,*" Victoria replied. Tim told Victoria he had to go, and they would discuss the situation further the next time they met.

Tim took the *Bright Red Toolbox* into the kitchen on Saturday afternoon. Bill was in the lounge room watching a movie on Netflix. Bill said, "What are you up to Tim," "Just looking for some clean polishing cloths to give the *Bright Red Toolbox* a clean, dad." Tim had been making so much noise, it was interrupting his movie. "There are some in the wash basket in the laundry, I washed them yesterday, just keep the noise level down a bit please." Tim grabbed a few micro-fibre polishing cloths, and a small old paint brush from the laundry, walking back into the kitchen to get the job done. Within a few minutes, the *Bright Red Toolbox* looked like new, not even showing the scratches from the time Tough Tommy hid it in the scrub, on the school camp in outback South Australia the previous year (Timid Tim and the Bright Red Toolbox go to High School). Tim put the *Bright Red Toolbox* back on the shelf in his bedroom. "See you later dad, I'm going for a ride on my bike," he said as he headed out the door.

"Don't forget we're having pizza for tea at 6pm," Bill reminded Tim.

Tim rode his Bright Blue Bike along the Murrimboola Creek wetlands. Although not quite a kilometre long, it was a great place to relax and improve one's mindset. Tim noticed a familiar face; it was Victoria sitting on the wooden bench seat. Victoria had tears streaming down her face, Tim, witnessing her sadness asked, "Are you okay? Can I help?"

Victoria wiped her tears away, "I need someone to help me, before I do something stupid."

Now it was Tim's turn to get emotional, "Victoria, I will do whatever it takes," his voice was quivering. There was a special calming, almost meditation mindset coming over the two teenagers.

Victoria became more confident, giving Tim the short version: "Sandra and her family left town in the latter half of last year," Victoria started. "I miss her. Sandra was the only person that cared about me, but I know she was also the person that got me hooked on the smokes."

"How did you go from cigarettes to vapes?" Tim asked. Victoria tried her hardest not to get upset.

"After the police had searched the house when we stole the smokes, mum and dad would search my room, but they allowed me to have the odd vape to reduce the withdrawal symptoms from the smokes."

"So that's how you got hooked on the vapes," Tim inquired. "Basically, you're right, but mum and dad were going through relationship stress, I would get stressed when they were arguing. In order to cope, I would steal a few dollars from mum's handbag to have my own supply of vapes."

"Was that to cope with your parents' relationship, or becoming addicted to vapes?" asked Tim.

Victoria explained: "A bit of both really, but once the addiction took hold, stronger than the original cigarette craving, it's taken me down a path I can no longer control."

Tim looked at the time, "Listen, Victoria, I have to go home now, but I don't like the idea of you being alone. If you don't have any plans, you could join dad and me for pizza." Before Victoria had time to reply, Tim said, "I don't know anyone in town and apart from my video games, it gets a bit boring sometimes."

Victoria replied, "It does sound like a cool idea, give your dad a call to make sure it's ok."

Bill set up some chairs on the small back veranda, he had cooked three varieties: Hawaiian, peperoni, and meat lovers. Tim and Victoria had a great time, deciding to defer the follow-up discussion for another time. Tim was

caught off-guard when his dad asked, "Is Victoria your girlfriend?" Both Tim and Victoria answered in unison "NO", then they then looked at each other and laughed. Bill apologised for his impromptu question. "Sorry for asking, but I have never heard of Tim having so much fun with a girl before."

Tim was embarrassed even more, saying, "Sorry, I need to be alone for a couple of minutes." before heading to his room. Bill looked at Victoria and said, "I stuffed up a good night, sorry."

"That's okay Mr. Bowman. Tim has been so helpful, being a good listener to me, so I could open up about my serious addiction to vaping. He probably saved my life today." Victoria then collapsed on the bare wooden floor. Bill rushed to her aid, yelling, "Tim, I need your help. Victoria had collapsed."

Within seconds, Victoria was okay again, "It's okay, I just have these anxiety attacks sometimes, Mr. Bowman."

"Please, call me Bill. I must admit you did recover rather quickly."

After re-assuring Tim that she was fine, Victoria said goodnight and walked home, taking her time to calm herself down.

Victoria apologised for what happened on Saturday when she finally caught up with Tim at lunchtime. "You did give us quite a scare, but I'm glad you seem to be a lot better. Do you think withdrawal symptoms, could be part of the cause?" Tim asked sympathetically.

"Definitely, but I need your help if I have any hope of giving up the vapes."

Out of the corner of his eye, Tim could see the gardener trying to get Victoria's attention. Whispering quietly to Victoria, Tim asked: "Is the gardener a serious part of the problem?"

Before Victoria had a chance to answer, the end of lunch bell rang. The positive vibe of Tim's support encouraged Victoria to ignore the gardener's gesture and walk with Tim to the next lesson. Victoria told Tim on the way to class how Graham Dennison, the gardener was the major problem while she was trying to give up the vapes. "Graham keeps pestering me to take the vapes, sometimes in exchange for introducing other students to start vaping and using him as the main supplier."

Tim said, "Don't worry Victoria, the *Bright Red Toolbox* will sort him out" as they separated, going to their own seats.

The *Bright Red Toolbox* comes to Victoria's aid

Bill woke up the next morning and suddenly smelt the bacon and eggs

Tim was cooking in the kitchen. Walking into the kitchen, Bill noticed the *Bright Red Toolbox* on the table. Tim saw his dad staring at the Bright Red Toolbox, "You hungry dad? Breakfast is nearly ready."

"I am actually, but what's with the *Bright Red Toolbox*?" Bill asked. "Victoria needs my help to deal with her vaping problem, and I think the *Bright Red Toolbox* might be needed," answered Tim.

Bill looked at the clock. "You had better get going then. Ride carefully with the *Bright Red Toolbox.* I hope it works as well as stopping the robbers at the Purple Lips Café."

Victoria was waiting for Tim at the bike compound, "Graham, the .gardener, is getting much worse," said Victoria after saying Hi.

"What happened?" asked Tim as he put the Bright Red Toolbox on the ground while he locked up his bike.

"Graham became angry when I told him *No* to any more vapes. He said, 'How am I going to get rid of all these new, stronger nicotine vapes?'"

Tim happened to notice that the *Bright Red Toolbox* was a brighter shade of red, almost an angry red. Tim looked at Victoria. "I'm glad I brought the *Bright Red Toolbox* to school, I think it's ready to go to work." Victoria said "I hope so Tim, I am so sick of this, I can't concentrate on my schoolwork anymore," as they headed to the classroom. Walking into the classroom with the *Bright Red Toolbox* created a bit of attention from the other students. Mr Harding wondered what all the commotion was as he entered the room to start the school day. "Mr. Harding, I brought along my *Bright Red Toolbox*, the guys were just a bit curious, I will put it away under the desk now," explained Tim.

Mr. Harding said, "That's okay, but we all need to direct our concentration to the lesson."

The gardener, Mr. Dennison, started to torment Victoria, trying to persuade her to buy some of the stronger vapes from him at morning recess. Tim was sitting at the usual spot. He had brought the *Bright Red Toolbox*, locating it in the centre of the table. The *Bright Red Toolbox* activated its rotor blades at the same time Tim heard Victoria scream "NO" from the direction of behind the building. Tim took the last bite from his sandwich, got up from his seat and followed the *Bright Red Toolbox*, with its rotor blades whirring, speeding towards Victoria's location. The *Bright Red Toolbox* would require a few extra tools for this important mission. The return to class bell rang out as Tim and the *Bright Red Toolbox* reached the escalating hostile situation. Graham Dennison, the gardener was being abusive towards Victoria, and four other unknown teenagers. Using the voice controller and speaker, the *Bright Red Toolbox* said, "Everyone stay calm, the situation is under my control until the authorities arrive." Graham started picking up the many boxes of vapes,

scattered about the ground where everyone was standing. It looked like Graham was intending to make a run for his escape. "STOP RIGHT THERE, LEAVE THE VAPES ON THE GROUND," echoed around the area from the speaker as the *Bright Red Toolbox* hovered in front of Graham. Tim and Victoria joined the four students they didn't know, preferring not to go back to class until they were sure Graham would no longer cause trouble.

The *Bright Red Toolbox* picked up one of the boxes of vapes using the robotic arm tool attachment. Sliding an unwrapped vape into the drug and chemical detection slot (one of the newest capabilities). While waiting for the results, the *Bright Red Toolbox* instructed the unknown students to advise the school authorities of the inappropriate behaviour, then go back to class. Graham was still in shock, and unsure what to do, witnessing the power the *Bright Red Toolbox* had resolving the precarious situation. Tim and Victoria hoped they wouldn't be in too much trouble, smiling to each other as Mr.

Harding arrived. The *Bright Red Toolbox* speaker announced, "Vape ingredients results are about to print out." Mr Harding asked, "What am I hearing about vapes?" as he watched the *Bright Red toolbox* hovering in front of Graham.

Graham knew he was in big trouble and tried to make another run for it. "Not so fast Graham, I have already called the police so stay and you will get a chance to explain your involvement." Mr. Harding continued, "Now, can someone please explain what is going on and how are you controlling the *Bright Red Toolbox*?"

"Mr Harding, Graham is to blame for supplying vapes to Victoria and many other students," Tim said as he began his explanation. Victoria and Tim looked at Mr. Harding, and they became a bit scared as his face became

nearly the colour as the *Bright Red Toolbox*. Mr. Harding looked directly at Graham and said rather loudly, "I want the truth Graham, NOW."

Graham was trapped by the *Bright Red Toolbox*, he was sweating profusely, a normal symptom for a guilty person. "I am very sorry Mr. Harding," Grahan said, showing signs of genuine remorse. "I started selling the vapes at the end of term four last year." Graham continued to describe the financial hardship he and his wife were experiencing due to the cost-of-living crisis.

"When I first started selling the vapes, I didn't know the dangers or how addictive they were."

Victoria couldn't help but interrupt, "Why did you have to put so much pressure on me after I clearly said no?"

"I am so sorry, Victoria, the bank is about to foreclose on the house. I need the money so my wife and I don't become homeless," Graham answered.

Tim walked over to the hovering *Bright Red Toolbox*, tearing off the vape ingredients list it had printed out. It was Tim's turn to speak: "Graham, take a good look at the list of harmful chemicals in the vapes you are selling."

The police arrived while Graham browsed the list of ingredients, He burst into tears, yelling out, "I'm so sorry," as the two detectives marched him off to the awaiting police paddy-wagon. The term paddy-wagon is said to be derived from the high proportion of early Irish settlers picked up after dark in horse-drawn police wagons. In years gone by, Patrick (Paddy) was one of the most common boys' names. Mr. Harding spoke to Tim and Victoria: "May I have the vapes and the ingredients list? Tomorrow, the entire class will have an educational day of the dangers of vaping." Mr. Harding wanted Victoria and Tim to be involved in the lessons, while the *Bright Red Toolbox* would be allowed for display purposes only. The end of day bell rang. Mr. Harding had already returned to the classroom to thank the relief teacher while Tim and Victoria were excused early and allowed to go home. They both said their goodbyes at the bike lock-up compound. Later, Tim was so tired, he placed the *Bright Red Toolbox* on the shelf in his bedroom, collapsed on the bed for a rest until teatime.

Tim met Victoria at the bike compound the following morning. Tim locked up his bike, then Tim and Victoria walked toward the classroom block. Tim carried the *Bright Red Toolbox* as they casually chatted about what happened the day before. Mr. Harding saw Tim and Victoria: "Can I see you both for a moment please?" he asked.

"No worries, Mr. Harding," they both said in unison. Mr. Broadbent, the principal, came over to join them. Mr. Broadbent introduced himself to the students: "Hi Tim and Victoria, Mr. Harding and I completed some research into the vaping problem in the state of NSW last night. The findings were quite alarming."

Mr. Harding then added: "We have put together an informative lesson as a way of making our students aware of the dangers of vaping." Victoria joined in the conversation: "That's a great idea, Mr. Harding. I would hate other students to go through what I have had to endure."

Once the normal early morning formalities were over, the students were informed about the vaping education training in the school library. The students made their way there whilst, some students muttered; 'What a load of rubbish,' under their breath. Victoria heard the comments but decided not to take any action. The students took a while to settle down, probably due to the sudden change in curriculum. Tim put the *Bright Red Toolbox* on the small table set up at the front of the lecture room. Mr. Broadbent and Mr. Harding entered the room carrying handout materials, instructing Tim and Victoria to pass the information to the students. A knock at the door interrupted the start of lesson. Mr. Akton, the school liaison officer, and substitute teacher, had heard about the information morning; "Mr. Broadbent, I heard about this anti-vaping session, could I attend as my appointments are this afternoon?"

"An excellent idea, we are just about to start," answered the principal.

Mr. Broadbent got the attention of the twenty-four students. "I would like to welcome you all here this morning, so that we can get an idea of the seriousness of vaping in Murrumburrah High School.

Students who have used a vape in the last few days, raise your hand please."

Eleven students cautiously raised their hands. Mr. Harding inquired: "I am sure there are a few more, but don't worry, no-one will be in trouble for their honesty." Three more students added to the tally. Mr. Broadbent grabbed a whiteboard marker and began writing the statistics on the board. "14 from 24 students equals over 58%". The students felt a bit more at ease as the lesson continued, handing over vapes in their possession on the promise of having them returned, even though in normal circumstances, serious consequences would be enforced. Open discussion was encouraged, this included Victoria describing the severe symptoms of withdrawal while trying to give up the vapes. The students chatted amongst themselves in a happy mindset as they headed off for morning recess break.

"I hope you all are more attentive after your recess break," said Mr. Harding. The students were asked to look at the information sheets as Mr. Broadbent took over the conversation. "While you were on break, we had the vapes you had earlier handed in analysed for ingredients." The principal explained even though four different brands were handed in, the ingredients were very similar to the list printed out by the *Bright Red Toolbox* the previous day. The students looked closely at the list of ingredients; PROPYLENE-GLYCOL, NICOTINE, MENTHOL, CLYCEROL, ACROLEIN, FORMALDEHYDE, DIACETYL, ETHYL-VANILLIN. They were not aware of many of the ingredients, or how dangerous they might be. Mr. Harding gave a mind-blowing lecture, describing the disturbing reason the manufactures put menthol in vapes: "Menthol increases the addictive behaviour of Nicotine."

After the vaping educational morning ended, the principal, Mr Broadbent advised the students that handed in vapes, would be returned as promised, but there was a catch; each student was handed a consent form, signing them up via parent/guardian approval to a vape and cigarette better health quit program. Mr. Harding announced how proud he was with the openness displayed during question-and-answer discussions. "Your positive behaviour has encouraged the school board to propose a similar vaping information program to be introduced throughout Murrumburrah High School.
"